# Copy Cat

Mark Birchall

Cat was small and Dog was big,
and whatever Dog did, Cat did too.

When Dog went dinosaur hunting,
Cat went dinosaur hunting with her.

Scrubbing Brush has never been on holiday before and is quite excited.

Granny's coming too. She has a new Young Pet called Truffles.

Scrubbing Brush thinks Truffles needs some Proper Training . . .

My goodness! Look at that —
it must be the Wide Ocean!

BIG AND SPARKLY

Traction Man and Scrubbing Brush
are exploring the secret crevices of the Rockpool.

Traction Man is wearing his Squid-Proof Scuba Suit,
Lightweight Shorts and Aquatic Air Tanks.

Who knows what creatures lurk
in this Underwater World?

If they stay very still
perhaps some of the
elusive Rockpool Animals
will appear.

Nearly everyone wanted to have a quick dip in the sea before lunch —

which leaves Traction Man and Scrubbing Brush and . . .

OPERATION PICNIC.

At all costs, this picnic must be defended against hungry Truffles.

No Truffles,
down boy,
keep back
from the quiche.

DIG DIG DIG

But Truffles must think Traction Man is some sort of bone and has carried him off.

Oh no! Traction Man has been buried for later.

Don't worry Traction Man, Scrubbing Brush has sturdy bristles and will dig you out in a jiffy.

Traction Man and Scrubbing Brush
are clinging onto a plastic bottle
in the vast sea.
They can hardly see land.

A colossal wave
towers
over them.

Traction Man is wearing
quite a lot of seaweed.

It's all dark.

Scrubbing Brush,
where are you?

Arf!

Thank
goodness!

Can you see that shape
in the gloom?

Keep very still Scrubbing Brush,
and don't be scared
(even though it has
hot breath
and dripping jaws).

But do you hear a voice?

What have you got there, Fluffy?

Traction Man and Scrubbing Brush are travelling by bucket . . .

Beach-Time Brenda™ Bucke

Well, we'll be going soon - but maybe he's been washed up further along...

Traction Man is in the Dollies' Castle, wearing seaweed hair and beard, a shell hat, a light dusting of sand and a floral sarong.
Scrubbing Brush has been garlanded too.
The Dollies are treating them to a feast of ice-cream and lollies.

. . . about this long,

wearing a red

scuba suit . . .

Look there, Scrubbing Brush –
do you recognise that nose?

I'm afraid your castle has been demolished
by Truffles the Puppy.
But don't worry, Traction Man and Scrubbing
Brush can help you rebuild it in no time.

Traction Man, Scrubbing Brush and the Dollies
are digging an exploration hole
to the Centre of the Earth.

(The Dollies are wearing Safety Jackets,
Excavation Shorts and Cave Helmets
borrowed from Traction Man.)

They have already unearthed
these buried treasures and the bones
of some ancient creature.

Behind them you can see
the Dollies' new castle.
They think it is Even Better than before.

Tomorrow they are all going to go
on an expedition to the Mysterious Cave
with their own lunch.

The Dollies have a dinghy . . .
and they are all
ready for
Anything.

Some other brilliant books by Mini Grey:

Egg Drop

The Pea and the Princess

Biscuit Bear

Traction Man Is Here

The Adventures of the Dish and the Spoon

Traction Man Meets Turbodog

Jim (by Hilaire Belloc, illustrated by Mini Grey)

Three by the Sea

TRACTION MAN AND THE BEACH (ODYSSEY)
A RED FOX BOOK 978 1 862 30815 2

First published in Great Britain by Jonathan Cape,
an imprint of Random House Children's Books
A Random House Group Company. Jonathan Cape edition published 2011
Red Fox Edition published 2012

1 3 5 7 9 10 8 6 4 2

Copyright © Mini Grey, 2011

Dedicated
to
TIA

When Dog balanced on the high wire,
Cat balanced on the high wire too.
"Copycat," said Dog.

When Dog went digging for pirate treasure,
Cat also went digging for pirate treasure.

And when Dog went deep-sea diving,
guess who went deep-sea diving with her?

So when Dog went to explore the Moon
and the planets and the stars, she made sure
that her spaceship had room for only one on board.

She didn't know that Cat had a spaceship just like hers.

"Copycat," said Dog. "Copycat, copycat, copycat! Why must you always follow me? You go everywhere that I go, and you do everything that I do."

The next day, when Dog went hunting dragons,
Cat wasn't there.

He wasn't there on the next day either,
when Dog went to discover the North Pole.

And on the day after that, Dog wanted to play soccer.
But where was Cat to play soccer with her?

"I wish I hadn't got so mad at him," said Dog.
"Sometimes it's more fun if there are
two of you to do things together."

And she went
to say 'sorry'.

"Come in," said Cat in the teeniest,
tiniest, most faraway voice.
There he was, tucked up in bed
and covered all over with spots.

"Oh, Cat, I was worried.
I haven't seen you for ages," said Dog.
"I never thought I'd miss you so much."

"I've missed you as well," whispered Cat,
"but I was too ill to come and see you."

"Never mind," said Dog.
"I'll soon make you better."

And she made him
special get-well-soup,
and gave him special
feel-better-medicine.

She read him exciting adventure stories,
until he fell fast asleep.

In the morning,
Cat felt good as new again.
He went to find Dog.

But she wasn't in the dinosaur park...

... or on the pirate island ...

... or on the moon ...

... or any of the other places that she liked to visit.

Where could Dog be?

"Copycat!" said Cat.
"Now it's my turn to make YOU better!"